The Blacksmith's Gift

By
Dan T. Davis

Illustrated by
Matthew S. Armstrong

Edited by Jan Davis

Second Star Creations

The Blacksmith's Gift
By Dan T. Davis
Illustrated by Matthew S. Armstrong
Edited by Jan Davis
Published by: Second Star Creations
12120 State Line Rd #190, Leawood, KS 66209-1254
http://www.secondstar.us
Email to: ordersBG@secondstar.us

Text copyright © 2004 by Dan T. Davis
Illustrations copyright © 2004 by Second Star Creations
Printed in China
First Edition

10 9 8 7 6 5 4 3 2 1
Publisher's Cataloging-in-Publication
(Provided by Quality Books, Inc.)

Davis, Dan T., 1957-
   The Blacksmith's Gift/by Dan T. Davis;
illustrated by Matthew Armstrong. — 1st ed.
   p. cm.
   SUMMARY: A childless carpenter builds a dollhouse for the blacksmith's daughter for Christmas — leading to the start of a legendary Christmas tradition.
     Audience: Ages 7-12.
     LCCN 2004091044
     ISBN 0-9725977-4-3

1. Christmas-Juvenile fiction. 2. Santa Claus —
Juvenile fiction. [1. Christmas — Fiction. 2. Santa
Claus — Fiction.] 1. Armstrong, Matthew (Matthew S.),
1975- II. Title.

PZ7.D2817B53 2004   [Fic]
                    QBI04-213

*Dedicated to
the child within all of us...*

"Mr. Kloss! Mr. Kloss!" shouted the agitated customer.

The bang, bang, bang of a hammer stopped from a room behind the counter. "Yes?" said a hidden voice.

"You promised me my wooden chair last week! I still don't see it anywhere among this clutter you call a carpentry shop. Have you even started it?"

Mr. Kloss stepped out behind the counter, emerging from his hidden workroom. He was a big man, with hands that showed he worked constantly with wood. He looked extremely tired, as if he'd been working all night. The rays of the early morning sun shone through his store window behind the customer, so he had to squint to see him.

"Err, no, it's not quite done yet, but I'll definitely finish it today. I've been working on some other projects that have a very high priority, which needed to be done sooner. You can understand that, I'm sure. But, I also understand your position. There won't be any charge for your repair. Will that be satisfactory?"

The customer appeared taken aback. "Free? Again? I don't like you being late, that's for sure, but if you keep giving me your services free because you're late all the time, then you won't make any money, and I won't ever get the work I need done!"

"Oh, it's no problem. It's my fault I'm behind, and you shouldn't suffer because of it. I'll make it up in the high priority projects that had to come before yours." The carpenter extended his large rough hand to the customer and the two shared a firm handshake. As the customer left, the bells on the door jingled loudly.

A woman's voice interrupted the bells. "They all do that to you, Papa. They say they don't want the work free, but all you have to do is be one day late, and they start screaming. We'll be in the poorhouse yet, even with all of your hard work." The carpenter's wife was also a big person, but one with grace and quiet sincerity. She had managed to appear at the doorway between the shop and the hidden back rooms without him even noticing.

"Ah, yes, Mama, I know, I know. But I had to work on the project for the wee one. When I start one of those, I always have to finish. You know that. But, come, come, and let me show you." The tired look left his face, replaced by a gleam in his eye. He lumbered past her into his workroom, expecting her to follow.

Yes, she knew. It had been like this for years. They were barely scraping by, on his carpentry work and her sewing for their small village. Life in Norway was hard, but life in Norway without enough money could be deadly, and winter was soon to come. They needed to make sure they had enough firewood for the cold months ahead, and she couldn't see it coming this year. He kept spending what little they had on supplies, and most of those supplies went toward his projects.

But she never could say anything when he showed his work. It was the only time she ever saw him truly happy.

"See, Mama, see! When the horse rocks back and forth, the bells inside the neck ring like it's Sunday!" He proudly displayed his latest creation, a small wooden rocking horse, already merrily painted with bright colors.

"So that was what he was working on last night," she thought. "Indeed, another project for the wee one."

She sighed, and a tear came to her eye. Having no children often made Papa extremely depressed. She couldn't fault him for once again spending the entire night making another wooden toy for their imagined child.

It wasn't practical, but she understood. Hadn't she herself sewn countless sets of baby clothes, just waiting and hoping for the day to arrive when she could tell Papa that he was to be a Papa in fact as well as in name? Even their names for each other had arisen from that hope. She no longer could remember why they called each other Papa and Mama, given they had never had any children, except maybe because of the animals they had raised and often became attached to. They usually ended up selling some of their animals to others, because they couldn't bear to eat the ones that they had raised for food.

She barely paid attention as Papa described his latest creation. He was pointing out the comfortable seat he had attached to the little rocking horse. As she stood in the doorway between the carpentry shop and the workroom, she glanced first at the door that led into their small living quarters, then toward the door of the storage room. She wandered past Papa and into the storage room.

"Mama?" asked the big man quizzically. He cradled the small rocking horse gently in his giant arms and followed her. The storage room was full, full of toys, full of things to play with. He had built toys for his imagined child of all ages, whether he was a seven-year-old with a carpentry set, or she was a girl of five playing with beautifully carved miniature furniture in an ornate wooden dollhouse.

He had already cleared an area for his latest creation. Each toy, every item, had a place of honor. But the shelves were full to overflowing, and it was harder and harder to find a place for a new one.

"Oh, Papa." She said it softly, but exasperatedly. "Look at you. Your hair is almost as much gray as red; your middle is growing every day. Look at me. I'm not much better. I'm getting old, getting wrinkles. We're too old now to have children."

"No!" said Papa. He placed the rocking horse onto the shelf as hard as one can possibly set down an object of reverence. "We're not that old! We still let the Lord know of our desire to have a child. Why do you say such things?"

She put her large arms around his big frame. "Oh, Papa. You're such a good man. But being good won't keep us alive and healthy. We already had to sell the horses. Maybe you should sell the carriage as well. I have to prepare for the hardest part of winter soon, and we don't have enough wood for ourselves, and not enough food for the animals in the barn." She didn't mention that maybe he should just work harder on his carpentry and charge for his work rather than often giving it away.

"You're right, Mama, you're right. Without horses, the carriage is of little use, and the metal on the tracks needs refurbishing. They don't slide well on the snow anymore. We don't go into the country-side much anyway, and we can meet our needs in the village. I'll see if the blacksmith would like to buy it from us."

Papa finished his morning tasks and gathered his things before leaving to see the blacksmith. Mama noted that he grabbed a handful of the candy brittle that she would make at his request so that he could have candy for any children he encountered on his way.

Mama knew not to expect him back for a while, since watching the children at play in the open village center was another one of the ways Papa coped with not having a child of his own. Everyone in the village knew Papa, and all the parents appreciated how he watched over their children. All the children knew and loved Papa as well.

Papa walked from his carpentry shop toward the blacksmith's, but naturally stopped at his well-worn spot on a bench where he could see the children. His supply of brittle was quickly gone once the children spotted him, and he laughed heartily as he gave each child a piece of the candied sugar.

His brittle exhausted, the children went back to their play. Papa watched them wistfully for a while, and then stood to leave for the blacksmith's shop.

In the thin layer of snow in front of him lay an abandoned doll. Nothing fancy, it was just a rag doll with sewn buttons for eyes, and a smile made of colored thread.

Papa picked up the doll and looked toward the children. None of them seemed to be concerned about having lost a doll. Papa looked closely at the doll and noted that it wasn't even clear whether it was a "boy" doll or a "girl" doll.

"You're like my wee one ..." he sighed. "I don't even know whether to make toys for a girl or a boy. I just have to guess, so I make both. Oh, I so wish you were here with me so that I could hold you and love you." Papa turned the doll to face the children. "You could go play with the children over there! See?"

A tear in his eye, Papa held the doll close to his chest. He watched as some of the parents came to claim their children so they could do their chores. He watched the parents, and as he often did, he said a prayer so that they would realize the precious gifts they had. He intoned to himself,

"Treasure your children …

love them with care …

the world would be different …

if they were not there …"

Papa stood with the doll and realized he was still cradling it in his arms. He felt a little silly, but he said brightly to the doll, "Shall we dance?" He held the doll out slightly and turned in a circle a few times as if he were dancing with his own child.

He stopped short as he almost ran over the little girl standing before him. Papa knew her, of course, Papa knew all the children. It was the blacksmith's daughter.

"Do you like dancing with my doll?" she asked.

"Do you mind?" asked Papa.

"No. I just think it's funny!"

"Would you like to dance, too?" laughed Papa. Upon seeing her enthusiastic nod, Papa carefully grasped her small hands with his large ones and all three of them danced in circles, Papa, the blacksmith's daughter, and the little rag doll.

After a few minutes, the giggling girl released a laughing Papa, and Papa bowed as he handed her the little doll. The girl curtsied in return, and ran toward her father, who had approached during the dance, but who had also politely waited until they had finished.

The blacksmith placed his hand upon his daughter's shoulder and said, "Can you run on home by yourself? Your dancing partner and I have some business to discuss." The little girl nodded and started running toward home, her doll safely in hand.

"That's right. We do!" said Papa, remembering his errand to try to sell the carriage. "But how did he know?" Papa wondered.

Later that day, Mama watched as Papa came back into the house. As he quietly removed his large coat and boots, he had the look of one who was both wistful and concerned. Sitting down to a meal of hot porridge, he said, "The blacksmith wasn't interested in the carriage, Mama. He had something totally different in mind. He asked if I could make him a set of wooden furniture with a wooden house for his daughter. I told him that such a task would be much work, and I didn't think I had the talent. He told me he knew it would take a lot of time, but if I could have it ready by Christ's day, that he would pay handsomely for such a treasure. Mama, he said he'd pay more than I make on ten projects!"

"That's wonderful!" said Mama. "We really need the money. And you already have made such a toy! You can have it ready for Christ's day without a problem!"

Papa reared up from his seat. The chair flew backward and landed with a loud thump on the floor. The porridge spilled all over the table. "Sell the wee one's toy? No! Never!" He stomped out of the room and toward the shop.

She started up after him. She paused, only to realize that she had little reason to speak, for she had been sewing yet another baby quilt, almost without thinking about it. She put the sewing on her chair so as not to be wet by the spilt porridge, and chased after him.

"Papa? Papa, where are you?" she asked, but knowing to head straight to the storage room. It was cold in there in the evening, and her breath came out a chilly white. Papa was hugging himself, partly for the cold, partly for the comfort.

"These are the wee one's toys!" His tone was almost one of desperation, of begging. "We must have toys for the baby. How can I sell such a thing?" He put his hands to his face to cover his tears.

She remembered how during the hard winter months two years ago he had built the dollhouse. It had taken him almost three months, and that was without the interruption of his carpentry business, for almost no items came in during the coldest Norway winter months. Although she had admired the dollhouse many times in the past, she was still amazed at the intricate detail, the miniature furniture in each room. It was truly a work of love. She understood how selling this would likely destroy his hopes; destroy his dream of their future family.

"Can you make another one for the blacksmith's daughter?" she said gently, taking his hands away from his face. "That would be for her, and not for the wee one?" She held him tightly, concerned as to how he would respond.

"I … I can try," he stammered.

Mama watched as Papa, trying to regain his composure, went out to feed the animals. She smiled, watching Papa as he looked furtively about, taking a new salt lick and walking away from the barn. She never quite understood why Papa seemed to want to do this secretly, as if he thought no one would know it was him who replenished the salt for the wild deer and other animals who used the lick.

Knowing Papa, she imagined that he had also put some grain into those large coat pockets of his to entice the deer to come to him. Mama inwardly laughed as she imagined Papa faced with the quandary of dealing with two or three deer at the same time. Papa was never able to decide which deer to offer the grain. He'd turn toward one with his offering, notice another deer, and turn to make the same offering to that one. Mama was sure Papa frustrated the deer with his attempts to please them all.

Mama's smile turned to a newly formed tear as she once again realized that Papa had that same problem with children. Papa simply had no ability to choose.

As they had grown older, Mama had occasionally hinted at taking a child into their home. Papa would either bristle against the idea or would throw out his hands in exasperation, saying, "But, Mama, there are so many children, which one would we take in? No, God will show us the child that belongs to us, you'll see. We will have our wee one."

Mama turned away from the window and went to clean up the mess Papa had made. Papa might be frustrated, but he was a loving, caring, wonderful man. When it came to children, deer, carpentry or relationships, Papa depended on God to make choices for him. Papa waited on God to grant him his wee one, in God's own good time. So, until God's good time arrived, they would continue not to have children, even though Mama knew that Papa would adopt all the children of the world if he could.

The winter winds and snows came, getting heavier and harder each day. Work on the dollhouse began to consume Papa, for little other work was to be done as the village settled in for the long winter. But Christ's day had only been eight weeks away when he had decided to take on the project, and Papa was not one to compromise on quality, especially not on a toy.

Still, on those very few days nice enough to actually get outside, Papa would watch the children in the park and bring them brittle.

After one such day, Papa was almost home when he saw that two boys were setting up the nativity scene at his small church in preparation for Christ's day. Papa smiled, because he knew that setting up the nativity was a rite of passage for these boys. They had finally reached an age where they were trusted to set up the scene by themselves, and they were obviously proud as they did so.

Papa approached and offered the two his remaining brittle. As they took some, he said conversationally, "That time of year again, is it?"

"Yes, sir!" they responded in unison. Proud to show their abilities, they continued to work as Papa watched. As one of the boys struggled to properly place the almost life-size statues of Mary and Joseph, he muttered, "These statues are old! Look, the paint is peeled off in lots of places."

"Yes, they are old, aren't they?" interjected Papa. Papa remembered lovingly carving the statues the year he had married Mama.

He had given them to the church that same year and was always proud whenever he saw them displayed. But as he gazed at the statues with the young boy's eyes, he saw that they were indeed in need of work, and that the years had not been kind to the paint which adorned them.

"I'll paint them again next spring." Papa added.

The boy stopped, realizing that he had been talking to the village's carpenter, and then he looked again at the wooden statues. "Oh," he said. "Sorry. They're nice statues. Really."

Papa simply smiled at the boy and gave him another piece of brittle. The second boy interjected, "I can't find the baby to put in the manger!"

"No baby," said Papa, quickly.

"What? Why not?" questioned the first boy.

"I cannot make such a thing," said Papa. "Only God's love can fill that manger. It is not something for me to do."

"Oh," said both boys, neither understanding. But they accepted Papa's word and filled the wooden cradle with straw.

Seeing the finished nativity set Papa to thinking about some miniature furniture that he wanted to make for the dollhouse, so he left the boys to continue work on his winter project.

The blacksmith came by once, maybe twice a week to observe Papa's progress on the dollhouse. The blacksmith was a good man, and always paid Papa, even when Papa was late with a project. And Papa was indeed going to be late with this one. The blacksmith admired each piece, every item that Papa would make. But, now, Christ's day was tomorrow, and Papa wasn't even close to finishing.

The blacksmith still had on his coat and boots as he said, "It's cold in here! Shouldn't you put more wood in the stove?"

"Yes, yes, I should," said Papa. "But I don't mind the cold as I work, and we're trying to save on wood. Money is tight, and the winter is long."

"Let me pay you for the work you've already done. Then you can buy more wood, food, and food for your animals. I've seen that grain you've been feeding them. It's old."

"I don't get paid until I finish."

"But it will take you another month to finish. I've dismissed the notion of having the dollhouse ready by tomorrow, but you should still be paid. You could use the money, and you've done good work so far."

"No. I'll get this done soon, I promise. I'll work on it day and night."

"You're stubborn. But I understand. I'll come see you next week or so. A good Christ's day to you."

"And to you." Papa shivered at the cold that rushed through the door as the blacksmith walked out of the shop. Talking about the animals reminded him that he needed to feed them, as night was coming on. Papa pulled on his heavy overcoat, covering the coat he had already been wearing. He pulled on his boots and went to the small barn to find some grain.

He almost cursed when he opened a new bag. It was indeed old. And though the grain bin was cold, the ambient heat from the barn had allowed this bag to become infested by grubs. Papa grabbed the bag and with his large towering frame angrily hefted it out into the snow. The force of his action burst the grub-infested bag and the contents were strewn across the whiteness.

Seeing the result of his anger, Papa fell to his knees and begged for forgiveness.

"Oh, Lord, I'm sorry. But nothing seems to be going right. The grain is bad, we don't have enough wood to finish the winter, I've had to slaughter more animals for food than I would have wanted to, and … and …"

Papa hesitated. He found it hard to put into words, even for the Lord.

"And … Mama … she told me today she thinks she really is too old now to have children. Why? Oh, Lord, you know we need a child. A child to love, a child to raise. My child. Can't you see how much I've done to prepare? How much we want one?"

The wind howled and the grain bin crashed shut. The noise interrupted Papa's reverie. He stood up, opened the grain bin, and was pleased to see that the next bag was grub free. And hopefully, that the grub ruined bag was the only one, since it had been apart from the others.

He hefted the bag over his broad shoulder, walked past the useless carriage, and went to feed the animals.

That evening, Mama lit candles for the Christ child. The two of them said their prayers, ate a small dinner, and went to bed. It had already been cold, but even with their thick comforters, Papa could feel it had gotten colder.

He got up, only to see that the fire, which he thought Mama had set for the night, had gone out. He went to find some more wood, only to find the woodbin empty.

Mama came up behind him. "I've been using some scrap lumber from your shop. We ran out of firewood yesterday, but with all your work on the dollhouse, I was going to wait until after Christ's day to ask you to go get some more. We should have stocked up more, but I'm sure we can get some more here in the village from those with excess. In fact, the blacksmith has a lot, I'm sure he'll give you as much as you want, given your work."

"I haven't finished the dollhouse." Papa stared at the dying embers. Almost no heat came from them at all.

"Well, I don't think there is any more scrap either. I couldn't find any tonight, which is why there wasn't enough wood for the fire. Come, come to bed. The comforter is warm enough, and we can find wood tomorrow. Even on Christ's day, I'm sure we can get some." Mama took Papa by the hand to lead him to bed.

"I won't be accused of being a beggar! And I won't have us without wood, not on the Lord's Day." Papa pulled away from Mama and began to quickly dress.

"But what, what are you going to do?" Mama was clearly perplexed.

"Just wait." Papa, now dressed, ran out of the living quarters. Mama followed him into the storage room. Papa was gathering up the dollhouse and its furniture. "Don't you see?" said Papa. "I'm going to let this dollhouse go to the blacksmith, and the one I am working on will be for the wee one!"

Mama smiled, having thought of this substitution weeks ago, but never having the courage to say it. Papa, bundled in his coats and carrying the heavy gift package with care, suddenly realized, "Do you think it's too late to go over there?"

"We retire early, and the blacksmith retires late. But for a gift like this, I don't think he'd mind being awakened even if he has settled in for the night." Mama looked outside. The snow had stopped, the moon was full, and the night was clear. She could see that a fire and lights were still shining brightly at the blacksmith's down the way.

Papa walked excitedly through the snow with his bundle. He set down the gift package and knocked loudly at the door. The blacksmith came and immediately welcomed him in. "Good evening! To what do we owe this visit?"

"I've brought a present for your daughter!" said Papa.

"What?" asked the blacksmith, clearly surprised. He whispered into Papa's ear. "It was still a month from being finished!"

"Consider it a miracle!" Papa laughed. "A miracle that I finished on time!"

He revealed the finished dollhouse and placed it in front of the little girl. Two other children, near the girl, also came up close to admire the work of art. All three oohed and aahed at each and every item. They quickly became absorbed in the craftwork and fun of the toy.

The blacksmith was astounded. "I don't believe it!" he said. "What can I do to repay you? I had given up on having this tonight."

"Oh, just some firewood for now. The payment can come when you can come by," replied Papa.

Papa saw that the blacksmith's daughter had left the other two children with the dollhouse and was now standing patiently next to him with her arms behind her back. He looked at her and smiled. She said, "Thank you so much for the dollhouse. It's beautiful!"

"You're welcome," said Papa.

"I have a present for you, too," she said. She pulled a rag doll from behind her and raised it toward Papa. "I know it's your favorite."

Papa took the doll, tears in his eyes. "I ... I ... don't know what to say ..." he muttered. "Thank you."

Papa turned to the blacksmith who simply smiled at Papa. The little girl returned to playing with the other children and the dollhouse.

Papa watched the three children play for a while. "Who are the other two?" he finally asked.

"I always have a couple of children from the orphanage in the next village come by during Christ's week. A little extra food and a little extra love never hurt," said the blacksmith.

Papa looked at the dollhouse and also looked at the doll in his own hand.

"But they should have a toy of their own ..." said Papa sadly. He placed the rag doll carefully into one of his large coat pockets. Suddenly, he brightened and said, "I'll be back!"

"What?" asked the blacksmith. It was too late. Papa had already left, running, huffing down the snow-covered road in the cold.

He rushed into the shop. Mama was sitting, still shivering. "Did the blacksmith's daughter like the toy, Papa?"

"Yes! But I'm not done." He went into the storage room and furtively looked around. Mama followed, and her look asked the question, "What's the problem?"

"I can't decide!" shouted Papa. "I can't choose! I need two toys for the other children!"

"What other children?" Mama asked.

"The children at the orphanage!" said Papa, obviously frustrated as he quickly glanced from one toy to another.

"There are a lot more than two children at the orphanage." Mama said matter of factly. "What do you mean?"

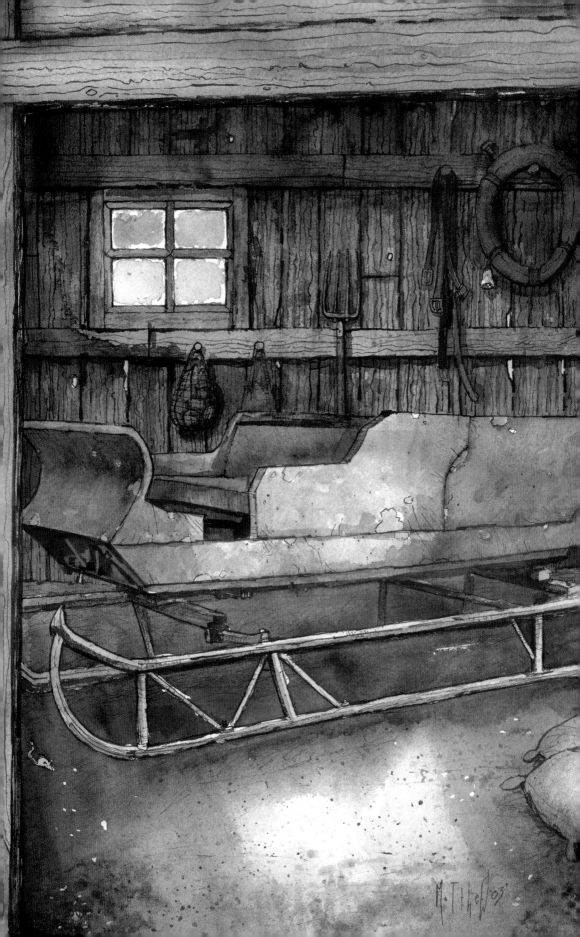

There are a lot more than two children at the orphanage.

Papa straightened, and stood like a statue for almost a minute. Mama watched him in silence. She knew when not to speak. Papa, without a word, began to pick up each toy, one by one, and began making trips toward the barn.

"What?" asked Mama.

"I'm loading the carriage," said Papa. "I'm sure the blacksmith will lend me his horses. He's a good man."

Mama instantly understood. "I'll go get the dolls, clothing, and stuffings I've made."

Back and forth into the house, the two began loading the carriage. Mama started to worry that it would be too full, as there were many toys and clothes that had been made and stored over the years.

At one point, Papa said, "I'll be right back, Mama."

He wandered off into the snow and Mama saw that he had gone to pray before the nativity in front of their nearby church. Mama sighed quietly and then continued to load the carriage.

Papa soon returned and saw Mama watching for him as he approached. As Mama turned back toward the barn, she suddenly exclaimed, "Look, Papa. Deer! An entire herd of deer is right outside the barn."

Papa stared into the moonlit darkness. Sure enough, he could make out the antlers of the deer. "They're eating the grain I threw!" he laughed. He had a strange urge to approach them.

Amazingly, they didn't run from him. "They're gentle as kittens!" he exclaimed to himself.

Realizing he needed to finish, he headed back toward the barn. Some of the deer followed him.

 "I've already finished, Papa." said Mama. "Go get the horses."

"I … I don't think we'll need horses, Mama. I don't know why, I just don't think we'll need them." Some of the deer were almost in the barn. Quietly, Papa began to hitch them up as if they were horses.

"Well, I don't believe it," said Mama.

Papa climbed into the sleigh, and the deer, antlers raised, silently led it down the road. Without a word from Papa, they stopped in front of the blacksmith's house.

The blacksmith, his wife, daughter, and the other two children were already outside in the cold, mouths agape. The blacksmith lifted the two orphans into the waiting carriage so Papa could hand them each a toy.

Papa winked at them all, and said, "Thank you. I've got to take all of these toys to the orphanage." He smiled at the two toy-carrying orphans as they joyfully left the sleigh.

The deer, again without a word, began heading down the road. So fast, that the blacksmith could barely hear Papa's shout of "Merry Christ's day to you all!"

The reindeer and sleigh disappeared quickly down the road. So quickly, they appeared to fly.

The three children stared quizzically up at the blacksmith. One of the orphans said to him, "Who was that? He was nice."

"That's our carpenter, Mr. Kloss," he answered.

"Santa Kloss."

Moonlight is
but a reflection of the sun.
Even so, 'tis Christ's day,
and the moon's light shines
upon a nativity
in the cold Norway night.

A time worn Mary and Joseph
smile upon the crèche.
And in that crèche is a baby.
A baby rag doll,
filling the cradle
with the love of God.

And near the crèche is a gift.
Not frankincense,
nor myrrh,
but instead, a toy.

A rocking horse,
with a hastily scrawled note
attached to the horse's neck.
The note says, simply,
"To my wee one"

Rock the horse …
if you do,
the bells inside the neck
ring like it's Sunday.

About the Author

Dan T. Davis has always loved creating new things. Computers and what they can do led him to build new technology businesses for Procter & Gamble, Universal Tax Systems, and Hallmark Cards.

Dan helped make world-wide e-mail a reality in the 1980s, allowed people to use the Internet to file income taxes in the 1990s, and designed ways for people to use their digital camera images to save their memories forever in the 2000s.

Dan's favorite activity is to create and design new ideas, new things, and new worlds. Here then, is one of those new worlds — the first of a trio of stories set in the best world of all: the world of the imagination.

Acknowledgements

No book is ever written without the help of others. First and foremost, I thank my wife Jan for always being there, and who is my anchor in this life. Thanks also to Akiko, my empathetic Sheltie, who jumps into my lap whenever I need a warm and generous hug.

As for the story itself, I thank God for the dream which led me to get up long before dawn to write the first version. Also, certainly, I thank family and friends. Their encouragement helped to make this book a reality. Finally, a thank you to Mark Crilley, the writer/artist of the comic book "Akiko", because through his work I found this book's illustrator. I love Matthew's artwork. I hope you do as well.

─────────────── *About the Illustrator* ───────────────

Matthew S. Armstrong was born on the ninth of June, 1975. Part of his childhood was spent in Whitefish, Montana. He still dreams of snowy forests and distant train whistles. This influenced the watercolors for this book immensely.

By day, Matthew works as a concept artist for Sony Computer Entertainment of America - drawing. By night he works on illustration projects - drawing. He draws a lot. He paints, too. Usually he draws before he paints; it's a lot easier that way.

Favorite things include but are not limited to: fine chocolate, unusual yet well crafted music, abandoned buildings with owls in them, certain shades of blue, nostalgia and robots.

Matthew lives in a little house near Salt Lake City, Utah with his lovely wife Isabelle and their year-old baby Claire. A year-old in 2004, of course.

─────────────── *Acknowledgements* ───────────────

Thanks to Isabelle who always lets me wake her up in the middle of the night to show her my latest painting. To baby Claire, who taught me nothing is real unless you bite it. I also thank my Mom who gave me my first drawing lessons. Also Amanda, Katie, Michael, Stephanie Burns, Earl, André, Phillip, Alex, Shannon, the other Andrée, Dominique and Madeleine. Lastly, to Dan, as this book wouldn't be here without all his hard work. I met Dan by chance and have decided it wasn't a coincidence. This is my second project with Dan. It won't be the last. You've been warned.

Second Star Creations

http://www.secondstar.us

Order Form

How to obtain *The Blacksmith's Gift*:

Publisher: http://www.secondstar.us

Email Orders: ordersBG@secondstar.us

Postal Orders: Send this form to:
Second Star Creations
12120 State Line Rd #190
Leawood, KS 66209-1254

Credit Card Orders: Check website listed above.

U.S. Orders:
$14.95 per book
Add $ 3 shipping/handling for first book, $ 1 for each additional book.
Kansas residents, please add 7.525 % sales tax.

Outside U.S. or want faster delivery?
Send e-mail or check web site for total charges.

Please print clearly.

Send me _____ copies of: *The Blacksmith's Gift*

Name: _____

Address: _____

City/State/Zip: _____

Phone: _____

E-mail: _____

My check or money order in the amount of $_____
payable to *Second Star Creations* is enclosed. (U.S. funds only)

Feel free to make multiple copies of this page!